Wrath
of the
Dragon

Marked by the Dragon Book 4

RICHARD FIERCE

Dragonfire Press

Cover design by germancreative.

Cover art by Nimesh Niyomal

ISBN: 978-1-947329-90-4

CONTENTS

MAP

1

Mina took a drink from her canteen and stared at the castle in the distance. It had only been two weeks since she'd left, and yet it felt like an eternity had come and gone since she'd last seen Klodian Keep. Gedrith and the other dragons wanted to go straight to the Dracan Dominion, but she asked them to stop here first.

Are you sure about this? Gedrith asked.

I think so. Lord Klodian needs to know what is happening.

Was it foolish of her to warn him? Possibly. The man had used her ability for his own gain, but he had also provided her with shelter and food. That wasn't a justifiable reason for her slavery, but she felt an odd sense of obligation toward him.

I'll be back as quickly as I can.

If you run into trouble, call for me.

I will.

Mina returned the canteen to her pack at Gedrith's feet and walked across the sand. She mulled over how Lord Klodian would react. Given her hasty departure, he probably thought she was dead. Thais probably did, too. And there was also the unresolved issue with Lady Burgess and the plot to overthrow Klodian. Had Thais handled that on her own?

The gates were open, and Mina walked into the courtyard. A quick look around showed nothing much had changed. She headed for the castle and was almost at the main doors when a voice called out behind her.

"Mina?"

She turned around to see Thais. The woman and had an astonished expression on her face.

"Where have you been? I thought you'd been taken by Lord D'Lance's spies."

"It's a long story," Mina replied.

"You can tell me later, then. Are you all right?"

"I'm fine. I need to speak with Lord Klodian. Is he here?"

"He is." Thais eyed her up and down. "You look like a soldier. Why are you wearing armor?"

"I don't have time to explain. Has anything odd happened around here?"

"Aside from your disappearing act?" Thais smirked and lowered her voice. "Actually, we might have a problem."

"Lady Burgess?"

"Yes. She left back to the Dracan Dominion after her husband reappeared with a strong sense of loyalty to Lord Klodian. He's still here, by the way, doting on Lord Klodian's every whim. She seemed deeply disturbed before leaving, but nothing has come of that situation that I'm aware of."

"Good. I had planned to help you with her, but I … got sidetracked."

Thais looked around to make sure nobody was nearby. "Does it have to do with that dragon you mentioned?"

Mina nodded.

"How did you escape?"

"As I said, it's a long story."

Thais glowered at her. "What's going on? You were trusting of me before you disappeared, and now you're being vague about things again."

"I'm sorry. There's a lot going on, and I don't have much time before I have to leave again. Lord D'Lance is doing more than just plotting against the High Prince. He's building an army of dragon riders."

"I know."

"You do?"

"I told you about why I'm here," Thais replied. "And there's a reason I believed you when you told me that dragons could talk. I've seen what he's done."

"Do you also know what he's doing with the dragon eggs?"

"Dragon eggs? I know nothing about that."

"It's bad, Thais. The dragons wanted to go to war with him, but I convinced them not to."

"How did you do that?"

"I have to kill him."

"Him who? Lord D'Lance?"

"Yes."

Thais laughed harshly. "Do you know what you're saying? Lord D'Lance is powerful beyond belief. If someone could kill him, they would have done it by now. And since when are you an assassin? You don't even know how to wield a sword."

Mina felt her face flush with warmth, but she kept her anger under control.

"Don't worry about me. Lord D'Lance may be strong, but I've got some mighty friends to help me."

"The dragons?"

"Listen to me, Thais. If I can stop Lord D'Lance, there won't be a war. With the dragons or the High Prince."

"If you want to commit suicide, go ahead. I won't stop you. You've changed, Mina. I don't know if that's a good thing."

Thais turned and walked away. Mina watched her go, wondering why she was so upset. If Lord D'Lance died, her parents would be free. Isn't that what Thais wanted? She pushed the thought away and entered the castle. Servants were going about their tasks, and the smell of fresh food drifted on the air.

It was such a busy atmosphere compared to the

dragon cave, which was normal for Klodian's court, but it was something that Mina had never considered before. She navigated her way through the maze of hallways, pausing outside the door of Klodian's personal chamber. There were two muffled voices engaged in conversation on the other side, and she was about to turn and leave when the door swung open.

"Keep me informed," Lord Klodian said to Captain Eduard.

Upon seeing her, they both froze. Mina offered a shy smile and offered a bow.

"My Lord," she greeted.

"I'll be on my way." Captain Eduard stepped around her and left.

"Am I seeing a ghost?" Klodian asked. "The last thing I heard was that you rode into the desert and your horse came back alone."

"I'm sorry if I caused you to worry. Can we talk in private?"

Klodian eyed her curiously and pulled the door open completely, motioning for her to enter. She stepped inside and waited to speak until the door shut.

"I must go to the Dracan Dominion."

"What are you going on about? You disappear for a fortnight and show back up, only to leave again? Do you know how many resources I used searching the desert for you?"

"May I speak plainly?"

"Please do."

Mina cleared her throat. Despite how strong she felt in her armor with a sword strapped to her waist, his presence was so imposing it felt as though she were still a slave under his control.

"Lord D'Lance is plotting to overthrow you."

Klodian's left brow rose, but otherwise, he didn't react.

"Explain."

"It's a lot to tell, but I overheard Lord and Lady Burgess talking. They mentioned that Lord D'Lance was going to request soldiers from the other Dominions and that you would refuse the request. That would give him what he needed to replace you as the ruler of the Thophate."

"And why would he want to replace me?"

"Because his goal is to take the throne of the High Prince."

"You've swayed my interest. Keep going."

"He's spreading rumors that Lord Culver and you are working together to cause a war that will divide the Dominions, and he's doing a good job of leaving convincing evidence."

"So you learned of this information two weeks ago and decided not to come to me directly?"

Mina flushed under his intense gaze. "I needed proof," she said. "I didn't want to make an accusation without it.”

“Fair enough. Where is your proof?”

“I don’t have anything physical to show you, but I trust the source who confirmed that it’s all true.”

“Who is this trusted source?”

Mina hesitated. This was where things were going to get tricky.

“Gedrith told me. He’s a dragon.”

2

Caden stood with his arms folded, watching the draman as they erected a line of new tents. Bast had done well with rallying their forces that had fled Velbridge after their failed attack. More of them had survived than Caden initially thought, and the presence of his master and her brethren continued to bring more draman to their ranks every day.

Lireth had been a constant presence in his mind ever since he'd freed her from the mountain. She listened to his every thought, but he didn't mind. The bond between them was stronger than anything he'd experienced before.

At her order, they had moved the camp further away from Velbridge to ensure Lord D'Lance's men didn't find them. Scouts had also reported that Lord D'Lance was no longer keeping it a secret that he had several dragons under his control. His patrols in the region had tripled, and there had even been sightings of his dragon riders keeping watch from the sky.

"It's impressive, isn't it?" Bast said. "I never expected to see so many of my brethren in one place, united under one cause."

"It is," Caden agreed. "But I can't help but wonder if it will be enough. We have Lireth and the others, but Lord D'Lance has more men in his army than the next two Dominions combined. Even without his dragons and the draman still loyal to him, we're outnumbered."

Bast stared at him, his pupils becoming thin slits.

"We may be outnumbered, but we have something more powerful than magic or steel, or even dragons."

"What's that?"

"Hope."

Caden shook his head. "Hope doesn't win wars."

"How do you know?"

"I've been in battle before. Skill and luck are the only reason a man walks off the battlefield alive."

"Do you go into battle wanting to die?"

"Of course not."

"You want to live, yes? You want to see more of this world, go home to your family?"

"Yes."

"None of that is a certainty. It's hope. Hope drives us more than anything."

Caden hadn't considered that before. He remained silent for a moment, then cracked a smile. "You are right. Forgive me. It is hard to see the sky for the clouds sometimes."

"We all have our moments of weakness."

"Leaders don't have that luxury," Caden replied.

"They should."

"I don't disagree, but not everyone views things the same way." Caden scanned the camp. "How many do we have now?"

"One thousand at last night's count, but we've probably had a hundred or more arrive just this morning. The idea of leaving secret messages that only the draman can see was a clever one."

"Sometimes I'm hit with genius."

They both chuckled. Caden felt his master's presence in his mind before she spoke, and he turned his gaze to the edge of the woods.

Come and speak with me.

"The master calls?" Bast asked.

"Indeed."

"Best not keep her waiting, then."

Caden left the camp behind and crossed out of the woods. Lireth and the other dragons kept to themselves, choosing to bask in the sun away from the trees. Considering how long she'd been a prisoner in the mountain, Caden understood her desire to be in the open.

He paused when he saw her. She was lying atop a pile of rocks, her massive wings outstretched. The sunlight glittered off her scales, a myriad of rainbows shimmering in and out of existence as her body moved with her breathing. Caden approached her and knelt a few feet from her head.

"I am here," he said.

I know. I can smell you even when you are in the woods. Humans have a particular odor to them I find hard to stomach. Yours, however, is manageable. Since we are joined, the scent is muted.

Caden wasn't sure what she was talking about. Joined? He shrugged the thought aside.

"What did you want to speak with me about?"

Straight to the point. That's one reason I chose you. Since you lead my draman, we have something to discuss.

"I'm listening."

Many in this world seek to do me harm. Lord D'Lance is the focus of my wrath for now, but there are others. I have received word from those in The Long Sands still loyal to me that there are rumblings among the Enclave. They know of Lord D'Lance's crimes against my brethren.

"What is the Enclave?"

They are the self-proclaimed leaders of the dragons. The metallic ones these days, anyway.

"So they are on our side?"

Hardly, Lireth hissed. *They are a worse enemy than Lord D'Lance, but I had not expected that I might need to deal with them now. If they come for Lord D'Lance, we will have to be quick.*

"I'm sorry, but wouldn't it be good to let them deal with him? If they are strong in number, they could clear out his defenses and leave him vulnerable."

Lireth retracted her wings and snaked forward. She snatched Caden up in her claw and brought him close to her face.

He will die by my flames!

Caden could feel the heat from her rage radiating off of her scales. He swallowed hard.

"Forgive me."

I must remind myself that you are a human, weak and unwise to the ways of dragons.

She snorted, her warm breath ruffling his hair, and set him down.

The Enclave is my enemy. They took many of my brethren captive, and hold them against their will even now.

"Do they know you are here? If so, their attack on Lord D'Lance may merely a ruse."

Now you are thinking like a dragon, Lireth said. *While I trust my servants, I also know that the Enclave may be feeding them information. We will keep our guard up and prepare for their arrival, but even if they do not come, we will face them in battle. Once I have killed Lord D'Lance, we are going to attack the Enclave.*

"You want to take the draman into the desert?"

Yes, and you will lead them. Together, we will tear down their archaic way of life and forge a fresh path. We will make this world bend its knees to us.

"You give me too much honor," Caden replied. "I will do my best to live up to your expectations."

If you don't, your end will come swiftly. I may have saved you from death, but I can give you back with a single breath.

Caden remembered the flames she'd spouted when he freed her. She was terrifying even when she was calm, and even more so when she was angry.

"I understand."

How many draman fill our ranks?

"Just over a thousand. We're growing so rapidly we're having trouble finding space for everyone."

That is a good problem to have.

"What of your brethren? Have any more of them agreed to come out of hiding?"

Lireth growled and scraped her claws on the stones beneath her.

Not yet. They fear the Enclave more than me. I will have to change that.

"Perhaps when they see Velbridge fall, they will change their minds."

That remains to be seen. Either way, they will fall into line or fall under my flames. Consider what I've told you and devise a plan for getting the draman to The Long Sands in one piece.

"I will."

Caden bowed to her and left, making his way

back to the camp. Lireth was full of rage. He understood why, but he feared that the path she was on would only lead to ruin.

Even so, he would follow her.

3

Lord Klodian's face creased with surprise, and then confusion.

"Did you lose your mind in the desert? Dragons can't speak."

"I didn't think so either, but I heard them in the mesa. The ones that attacked you and killed Vhan. They aren't wild animals at all. They're just like us."

"I'll admit, you had me in the beginning. The idea that Lord D'Lance would want the throne isn't outside the realm of possibility, but the rest of your prank borders on the imbecilic."

"This isn't a prank," Mina protested.

"Then you have lost your sanity, especially if you expect me to believe something so outlandish."

"I've been with them in the desert. They have an entire cave system underground that serves as their home. The things I've seen … you wouldn't believe me. But I assure you, my Lord, my wits are still intact. The scale in my leg belongs to Gedrith. He and I share a bond that allows us to communicate with our minds."

Lord Klodian's expression turned to one of scorn.

"You sicken me," he said. "If what you say is true, then you are worse than a slave." His fists clenched at his sides.

"Whether or not you want to hear it, it is the truth. And I'm telling you because I felt that you should know what Lord D'Lance is plotting. Do with the information as you will, but know that I am going to kill him."

He laughed at her, just as Thais had.

"You won't get within a hundred yards of him before his Runesmen tear you apart."

"If I don't succeed, then the dragons will go to war against him and ravage everything in their path."

Lord Klodian shook his head.

"Get out."

Mina wasn't completely surprised by his reaction, but she had hoped that he would be more receptive. She gave him a nod and left the room. There was nothing else to be done. He knew of the threat that Lord D'Lance posed. What he chose to do about it wasn't her concern. She went to her room and found her belongings were still there. It surprised her that the servants hadn't thrown everything out.

Her clothes were old and tattered, so she didn't bother packing them. She slid the chest of dragon horns out from under the bed and opened it, gazing at them. Each one came from a dragon that had lost its life because of her. Knowing what she did now, the collection gave her an ill feeling in her stomach. She closed the lid and hefted the chest. It was the only thing she was going to take.

As she walked through the castle, the servants and nobles gave her looks of curiosity. They probably all thought they'd lost her to the desert. A smile crept across her lips. Let them talk. Let them wonder.

She exited the castle and walked through the courtyard, taking a last look at everything. She'd grown up here, and she had a bittersweet feeling about leaving for good. Of course, she didn't know if it was permanent, but she suspected that once she reached the Dracan Dominion, her entire life would be different. If she survived her encounter with Lord D'Lance, anyway.

Gedrith watched her approach and she could smell freesia. She dropped the chest onto the sand and looked up at him.

This is a mark of shame.

Gedrith snaked his head down near it and sniffed the air.

It stinks of death.

Mina swallowed hard and nodded.

It's the horns of the dragons who've died because of me.

Why do you keep them?

It was a way to make myself feel better about being a slave. Every dragon that died was one step closer to being free. Or so I thought, before I met you. I brought them out here because I want you to burn them.

Do you think that will absolve you of your guilt?

No, she answered. *Nothing ever will. This is going to haunt me forever.*

Gedrith hummed in reply, his tail swishing across the sand.

Move away.

She did as he asked, moving to stand beside him. He opened his jaws and released a stream of flames that set the chest on fire. Mina watched it burn, and in a way, she felt as though it was her past that was burning.

Did you speak with Lord Klodian?

Yes.

I assume it did not go well.

No, it did not.

Are you ready to leave, then?

Mina grabbed her pack off the ground and climbed up his shoulder, settling onto his back.

Let's go, she said.

Gedrith launched into the air and flapped his powerful wings, taking them high above the landscape. The other dragons joined them, flying in formation behind Gedrith. Once Mina could no longer see Klodian Keep, her mind eased.

Have you been to the Dracan Dominion before?

Yes, though it has been a long time.

How long?

It was before Maël's betrayal.

Then you are going into this as blind as I am.

Humans like to expand and build, so I am sure it will differ greatly from what I remember.

We'll need somewhere to stay that is away from prying eyes, Mina said. *If anyone sees you or your brethren, they could alert Lord D'Lance.*

I know of a place that should be safe. It was once home to a dragon I knew before the colors turned on one another. It should serve our needs.

How do you know they don't live there anymore?

A hint of saffron hit her nostrils, but it quickly faded before she could pinpoint the emotion behind the smell.

I know because she abandoned it. The last time I came to the Dracan Dominion, it was to capture her.

Why would you capture another dragon?

She was the one responsible for the division between the colors. She gathered the chromatic dragons and sided with Maël. When the elders learned of her betrayal, they wanted to imprison her. When I came to get her, she was gone. The cave hadn't been lived in for some time. Not even her scent remained.

Is she still alive?

I don't know, Gedrith replied. *I never found her. She was a mighty dragon even then, so it is likely that she is not dead.*

You said you knew her. Was she your friend?

There was a long pause before he answered. *Yes. Once.*

Mina could sense a wall of turbulent emotions behind his words, so she didn't press for more information. They flew in silence for a long time, so long that Mina's eyes began to droop. She jolted several times, startling herself into wakefulness.

Are we almost there?

Yes. Do you see the castle to the right?

Mina squinted and saw a gray splotch, but the details evaded her.

Somewhat.

That is Lord D'Lance's fortress. The cave we will use is a few hours' walk from it. We could get closer, but we might be seen. If we haven't been already.

Mina looked down and watched the scenery speed by. If anyone was down there looking up, she couldn't see them. Trees came into view, and Gedrith began his descent. He glided over the canopy until the treetops thinned out to a clearing, then he swooped down and landed. Mina climbed down and stretched her muscles.

Where's this cave at?

That way. He nodded toward the other end of

the clearing. He sniffed at the air, his head swaying from side to side.

What is it?

I'm not sure. I've smelled nothing like it before. Stay here. My brethren and I will scout ahead to make sure there's nothing to worry about.

Gedrith launched himself back into the air, joining the other dragons who had yet to land. They circled over the clearing, then broke formation and each headed in a different direction. Mina rolled her neck, trying to work the kinks out. She scanned the tree line and saw something metallic flash.

A moment later, a monster stepped into the clearing.

4

"We have a few problems," Bast said to Caden as he returned to the camp. "We're running out of supplies. The last of the tents have been assigned, and we still have two dozen draman that need shelter."

"Divide them across some of the others until we can get more," Caden replied.

"We're also running out of food."

"How? The woods are full of deer and other animals."

"It seems our growing presence here has driven the wildlife away. I've sent scouts further out, but they aren't having much luck."

Caden frowned and ran his hands over his face, scrunching his eyes closed in thought.

"We could send some men to Velbridge to buy supplies."

Bast snorted, his reptilian nostrils flaring wide. "It will take a lot of coin to feed this lot."

Caden was well aware of their lack of funds. It seemed as though their problems continued to grow just as quickly as their numbers did. He knew this day would come, but he hadn't expected it to happen so soon.

"Do you remember what we discussed about

Lord D'Lance's caravans?"

Bast grinned. "Yes."

"It's time to set that plan into motion. Put together a group of draman, no more than ten or twelve. You and I will lead them on a trial run. It'll give us the supplies we need and give him a few headaches."

"As you command." Bast walked away to gather their crew.

Do not draw him down upon us, Lireth warned. *We are not ready yet.*

"I won't," Caden said aloud, unsure if she could hear him. He wished he could communicate with her as she did with him, but so far, the ability eluded him. Still, she could read his every thought, so he visualized the words in his mind.

Within an hour, Bast had gathered a group together and he and Caden led them through the woods to the nearest road. Scouts were posted at strategic points, providing updates on the movement of shipments coming and going from Velbridge, and they had noticed a pattern.

"You're sure that it's today?" Caden asked.

"Yes," Bast replied. "And always at the same time."

"Good. Make sure everyone is hidden. I'll get the wagons to stop, and at my signal, that's when they should reveal themselves. Keep an archer ready in case any of the drivers try to make a run for it, but they shouldn't shoot to kill. We want to send a message to Lord D'Lance and we can't do that if everyone dies."

"We'll be ready."

Caden sat on the ground beside the road and waited. Eventually, the clopping of horses and raised voices reached his ears. He waited until the wagons came into view and counted three of them. They rolled along the road, no guards visible.

Good, he thought. *This should be painless.*

As the wagons drew closer, he stood up and moved onto the road, raising his hand to the lead driver. The man was looking off into the woods, and for a moment, Caden thought the driver had spotted the draman.

"Hail!" Caden shouted.

The driver snapped his gaze forward and jerked on the reins, forcing the wagon to a halt.

"Get out of the way! I could have run you down!"

"Sorry about that. I'm in need of some help. Are you headed to Velbridge?"

"Aye, but we don't have any extra room. You're welcome to join us on foot, though you could walk there yourself without us."

"You're right about that, but I haven't had a meal in days," Caden lied. "Do you have anything to spare?"

"A beggar, then? Move aside. I don't have time

for this."

Caden whistled. A moment later, Bast and the others stepped into view. They all had their hoods down, leaving their reptilian faces in plain sight.

"Apologies, friend, but we'll be confiscating your goods. You can keep your wagons, we just want what's in them."

"Lord D'Lance will hear of this!"

"By all means, let him know. And also tell him that Caden Davtyan sends his regards."

The draman moved in and started rifling through the wagons. Terrified cries filled the air, and Caden heard the words "demon spawn" mentioned several times. Bast approached him, shaking his head.

"There's more here than we can carry."

"We'll unload it and carry what we can back to the camp. Two draman will stay behind with what remains and we'll come back for it."

"Is that wise? Lord D'Lance may have his patrols out here by then."

"Good point," Caden said. "We'll hide the rest and come back when it's safe, then."

"I'll let them know what to do."

Caden turned back to the lead driver, who stared daggers at him.

"You must know that you serve a tyrant."

"Lord D'Lance is a generous man with a heart

for his people," the man replied. "The only thing you're doing is hurting me and my family. You're stealing from *me*, not Lord D'Lance."

"Are you not taking these goods to Velbridge for Lord D'Lance?"

"I am."

"Then we are stealing from Lord D'Lance."

"It's only theft if it's paid for," the driver retorted. "I don't get paid until I deliver. When I show up empty-handed, I won't get anything for my trouble. So again, you are stealing from *me*."

Guilt assailed Caden. He didn't want the innocent to suffer, and surely not by his hands. He looked at Bast. The draman was helping the others unload sacks from the last wagon, stacking them in a pile. He was torn. His men needed to eat, but this man's livelihood was at stake.

Steel your emotions, Lireth bade. *There is no room for a conscience during war.*

His first instinct was to argue, but his discontent was pushed aside, suffocated under the weight of her presence. Caden gritted his teeth and reached for the bag of coins at his waist.

Don't.

Lireth's word was a command. If he defied her, she would kill him. He didn't want to disobey her, but his morals battled against his loyalty. Caden clenched his hand into a fist and turned his back to the driver. He tried to tell himself that what he was doing was more right than wrong, but he wasn't convinced.

"We're done," Bast said. "Everything has been unloaded. We'll be able to feed the camp for a few days with all this."

Caden's eyes roamed over the pile of stuff they'd taken. There were sacks of grain and rice, as well as wicker baskets full of fruits and vegetables.

"Leave," Caden said, turning around to face the driver again. "And be sure to tell Lord D'Lance what I said."

The man shook his head and flicked the reins. The horses pulled forward, and the wagons continued toward Velbridge. In the back of the last wagon, the head of a small child peered out from the covering.

"This is wrong."

"Is it? We're able to feed ourselves. Seems well and right to me."

"I suppose," Caden grunted, but it still conflicted him. "Let's get this stuff off the road."

He helped the draman carry everything into the woods and they covered what they couldn't transport with brush and leaves. By the time they returned to the camp, Caden realized that Lireth's presence seemed far away. He handed his supplies off to one of the draman and looked around the line of tents.

"Sir," a breathless draman rushed over to him.

"What is it?"

"Dragons have been spotted."

"More of Lireth's brethren?"

"No, sir. They are the metallic colors of her enemy."

Caden sprinted out of the woods to where Lireth had been earlier.

She was gone.

5

Mina watched the creature in disbelief. It walked on two legs like a human, but its appearance was reptilian. She remembered what the Enclave leader had said about Lord D'Lance mixing dragon eggs with humans to create an army. Although she knew the dragon hadn't been lying, it still shocked her to see one of the things up close.

She was in the open, and before she could try to hide, the creature spotted her. It shouted something and ran toward her. Mina drew her sword and took a defensive stance. She sidestepped the creature as it reached her, his sword cleaving the air harmlessly. The facial features looked masculine, and she assumed it was a male. He struggled to stop his momentum, and Mina stepped behind him and landed a blow to the back of his knee with her foot.

It surprised her when the creature didn't fall. His leg didn't even buckle. He whirled around, snarling. She backpedaled and swung her sword at him, but he blocked the strike with his arm and her blade clanged as if striking metal. Her brow creased in confusion and the creature took advantage of her surprise. He grabbed the blade of her sword with his clawed hand and jerked it free, tossing it aside.

Mina made a dash for the weapon, but the creature crashed into her, the two of them landing on the ground in a tangle. He was larger and stronger than her, and he quickly gained the upper hand and pinned her down.

"Yous is mines now," it said.

Help! Mina pushed the plea through the scale.

The creature leaned in close, and she could smell his foul breath. It stunk like rotten eggs. She turned her head to the side, struggling to break free. The creature laughed, droplets of saliva landing on the side of her face.

Gedrith!

A shadow passed overhead and the creature looked up. Mina tried to pull her arms free, but the creature gripped her flesh tighter and growled. He stood, pulling her to her feet and wrapped his right arm around her neck. Mina scanned the sky, but there was no sign of Gedrith or the others.

The creature drug her backward toward the tree line. She stared at her sword, wishing she could magically command it into her hand. A roar split the air, and she jerked her head in the direction of the sound. She still didn't see any of the dragons, but Gedrith's presence was strong, which told her he was nearby.

A glance over her shoulder revealed the creature's uneasiness. His eyes were wide, and he kept growling lowly. He was distracted. Mina did a silent countdown and then broke free and ran for her sword. The creature chased after her, but she managed to grab her sword before he reached her. She jabbed the blade forward, striking the creature in the chest, but it did no harm. Was the beast impervious to weapons?

A whooshing sound filled the air as Gedrith swooped down out of the sky and snatched the creature up in his claws, crushing him. He flung the body into the trees and landed.

Are you hurt?

No, I'm fine. What was that thing?

They call themselves draman. Neither human nor dragon, but a mix of both.

How do you know what they are?

My brethren and I just killed an entire group of them. One was so frightened, he babbled on about many things before I silenced him. There are more of them out here, so we need to be vigilant.

Mina sheathed her blade and tucked her hair behind her ears. She was about to say something when a deafening roar echoed across the clearing. She clapped her hands over her ears, looking to the sky. An enormous black dragon landed in the clearing, snarling with fury. Dragon fear washed over Mina and she fell to her knees, but she managed to crawl behind Gedrith.

The copper dragon wrapped his tail around her, keeping her in place as he turned to face the black behemoth.

So, it is you *that slaughters my children. I should have known the Enclave would stoop to murder.* The dragon's voice echoed in Mina's mind.

Those abominations are yours? Gedrith replied.

Have you sided with Lord D'Lance as well?

The black dragon snorted. *Do not mention that name to me. I will burn his castle and everyone in it.*

Mina gasped at the thought of Caden being burned alive.

Who's the welp?

She is my bonded. The first rider in a thousand years.

I wouldn't be so sure of that.

The only true rider, Gedrith clarified. *Those twisted bonds that Lord D'Lance has created were not forged willingly.*

Who said that's what I was talking about? But it does not surprise me that the Enclave knows about his dealings. They've never kept their snouts to themselves.

You allied with Maël knowing his course was only about greed. Do not defame the Enclave because you made a foolish decision.

What do you know about me, Gedrith? Nothing. Did I want more for our brethren? Yes. Count me guilty of that desire, but you are confused when it comes to what is right. Was it right for the Enclave to imprison our own kind?

They made their choice to join you in your folly, Lireth. They are just as guilty as you.

Lireth growled. *What are you doing here? Are you leading the Enclave to war against the humans?*

There will not be a war with humans. My bonded will slay Lord D'Lance and put an end to his blasphemous acts.

That scrawny human is going to kill him, is she? Not if I get to him first. He and I have history, and my vengeance is coming.

Then we are united in our cause. Perhaps if you help us against Lord D'Lance, the Enclave would forgive your past deeds.

Do not waste your words on me, Gedrith. Once I have killed the human, I am coming for the Enclave. No one is safe from my wrath, least of all our brethren.

I cannot let you leave knowing that you are going to attack the Enclave.

Are you challenging me?

Gedrith released Mina.

Go into the woods, he said.

Mina nodded and sprinted for the trees, dragon fear weighing heavily on her. She reached a tree with a thick trunk and stood behind it, peering out cautiously. The two dragons circled one another, their tails flicking back and forth behind them. They were equal in size, though Lireth's wings were larger.

The other dragons that had come with them appeared over the clearing, dropping down to surround Lireth. The Enclave had sent five dragons with them to terrorize Lord D'Lance's forces, and all of them were silver. Gedrith had told her silver dragons were the fastest of the metallic colors, and having seen them in flight herself, she knew it was true.

Mina's heart thundered in her chest as she watched. She expected to smell the scent of lavender from Lireth, but instead, she only caught hints of rose and saffron. They outnumbered her. Why wasn't she afraid?

A battle cry erupted from the other side of the clearing and a host of draman swarmed forth from the trees. A man was with them, a human, and Mina's eyes widened in surprise. No, it couldn't be. She gasped.

It was Caden.

6

"She's just up there!"

Caden led Bast and a contingent of draman into a clearing where he spotted Lireth. As soon as he'd been told that they had seen her enemies in the area, he knew there was trouble. He couldn't explain how, but he knew exactly where to find her. As they entered the clearing, Caden skidded to a stop.

There were six other dragons. Five were silver and one was reddish copper. He was just as monstrously large as Lireth, and the metallic dragons had surrounded his master. The sight of so many of the beasts made his knees go weak and fear paralyzed him. He watched helplessly as the draman swarmed forward, attacking the enemy dragons. It was like watching ants try to take down a tree.

The copper dragon swatted the draman aside and rushed toward Lireth. She roared and backed up, swiping her massive claws at him. She missed and the two of them clashed. Caden remained frozen in place. He screamed at himself within his mind to do something, to help his master, but what could he do against dragons? He would surely die. And yet, he would rather die defending his master than watch her fall to her enemies.

Caden used every ounce of mental strength he could muster and pushed through the fear. He staggered forward a few steps and drew his sword, then paused. Would steel even pierce the scales of a dragon? Probably not. He sheathed the blade and ran to a draman that was lying on the ground. It wasn't moving. Caden looked into the draman's open eyes and there was no life in them. He glanced around and saw that several others were also dead.

Lireth and the copper dragon were still fighting, a rolling ball of vicious talons and snapping teeth. The silver dragons stood by impassively, ignoring Caden and his men. Bast was helping a limping draman to the tree line, and he glanced over his shoulder at Caden. Once the draman was out of danger, Bast returned and joined him.

"Our master is outnumbered."

"We need more men," Caden said.

"No," Bast replied. "We do not have enough to defeat a single dragon, let alone six."

"We have to help her."

"Yes, but how?"

Caden didn't have an answer. How indeed?

"What's a dragon's vulnerable spot?"

Bast remained silent. The copper dragon gained the upper hand and pinned Lireth down, clamping his jaws around her neck.

"Hurry!"

"Without a weapon crafted of magic, the only weak spot is the eyes," Bast answered. "You'll be burned alive before you get close enough to try anything."

"What about arrows?"

"No. Even if you had the marksmanship to hit a dragon in the eye, arrows are too frail to puncture the membrane that covers the eyeball. A sword could do it, but as I said—"

"Save your words, my friend. They'll not sway me. You're in charge. If I die, do whatever you can to save her."

Caden sprinted toward his master, dodging between the silver dragons that surrounded her. He climbed up the copper dragon's tail and ran along its back. The beast jerked and Caden almost slipped, but he grabbed onto the dragon's scales and forged ahead. The dragon flexed its wings, trying to push him away, but Caden dropped on all fours and kept going. He reached the dragon's neck and stood, quickly drawing his blade. If he could just strike the creature in one of its eyes, his master could get free.

Before he could take another step, the dragon released Lireth and rose into the air, standing on its back legs. Caden scrambled to grab ahold of the dragon, but his hands slipped off the scales and he fell, landing hard on the ground. The impact forced the air from lungs and stars burst before his vision.

Free of the copper dragon's jaws, Lireth got up and leaped into the air, escaping. The silver dragons started after her, but the copper dragon roared at them and they stayed put. As Caden fought to gain his breath, the look in Lireth's eyes flashed within his mind's eye. She was afraid, but of what? The copper dragon, or of being imprisoned again?

The thought fled his mind as the copper dragon turned to face him, its clawed hand clamping down around him. He was going to die. There was no doubt about that. But he had ensured his master escaped, and so he had done his duty. He closed his eyes as the dragon's face drew down upon him.

"Stop!"

It was a woman's voice. Footsteps approached, but he dared not open his eyes. He waited expectantly to feel pain, but nothing happened. A few seconds passed, and the dragon's weight lifted from his body. He cracked his eyes open and saw a woman standing in front of him. She was facing away from him. Her hair was long and blonde, and she wore armor and carried a sword at her side.

She finally turned around, and his eyes widened. It was Mina! His excitement quickly faded. She couldn't be here, not really. Either he was hallucinating, or … he was dead. Yes, it had to be the latter of the two. Mina knelt beside him and peered into his eyes.

"Caden? Can you hear me?"

Her voice was the same as it had been in life. He smiled at her.

"I know this isn't real," he gasped. "But I don't care."

"What's not real?"

"You. This. Everything."

Mina laughed. "It's all real," she said.

"Even you?"

"Yes. Here, let me help you up." She offered her hand. Caden accepted it and she pulled him into a sitting position, then onto his feet. The dragons towered over him, death in their eyes. He spotted his sword on the ground and made a move to grab it, but the copper dragon's growl stopped him.

"He will not hurt me," Mina said, casting a look behind her. "Here." She retrieved the sword and handed it to him. Caden hesitantly accepted it and sheathed it.

"What's going on? Are these creatures keeping you against your will?"

"Hardly. They are my protectors. Well, these ones are." Mina waved at the silver dragons, then thumbed behind her. "This one is my friend."

"Friend?"

"Yes. His name is …" She paused. "Copper. He and I are bonded."

"I don't understand."

"You hit your head pretty hard when you fell. You should probably sit back down."

"I'm fine," he said. "I'm just confused. You said you were bonded to a dragon. What does that mean?"

"We can talk to each other using our minds, among other things. I know, it's a lot to take in."

Caden looked from her to the copper dragon. They could communicate using their minds? That was how Lireth spoke to him. The similarity startled him. Did that mean that he was bonded to Lireth? He could feel her presence, but she wasn't close by.

"What are you doing here?"

"It's a long story," she replied. "Why did you attack Copper?"

"Because he attacked my master."

Mina's forehead creased. "Your master? Do you mean Lord D'Lance?"

"No. That tyrant can burn for all I care. I'm talking about Lireth."

"The black dragon?"

"Yes."

Mina's expression fell. "Oh. I have some bad news."

7

Mina stood beside Gedrith and watched Caden as he paced the clearing. The other dragons had gone into the cave after Gedrith told them not to pursue Lireth, and Mina told Caden about his master's history with Gedrith and the Enclave. She supposed he was feeling conflicted about where his loyalty resided.

He cannot be saved, Gedrith said.

Why do you say that?

Lireth is the most deceptive dragon I have ever known. If she has bonded to him, she is fully ingrained in his mind.

Can a bond be broken?

I have never known one to be severed except by death.

Mina had a sinking feeling in her stomach. Caden was her friend, and she previously entertained the idea that they could be more than that, but if what Gedrith said was true, then she didn't know how their paths would end up.

When you lost Lucius, how did it feel?

Like I had lost a part of me, Gedrith replied.

Does it feel the same for humans?

Yes. I think that is why Areg has stayed with us all these years. Being with us must bring him solace from the pain. It is said that time heals all wounds, but that is not always true. Some wounds never heal.

The pain behind his words tore at her heart. She rested a hand on his foreleg comfortingly. Caden stopped walking in circles and turned toward her, striding purposefully.

"Can I speak with you?" he asked. "Alone?"

Gedrith growled.

It's all right, Mina reassured him. *Caden would never hurt me.*

So you say. You don't know Lireth or what she's capable of.

I'll be fine.

Mina joined Caden, and they walked together through the woods until Gedrith was no longer visible.

"I want to apologize," he finally spoke.

"About what?"

"For kissing you at Klodian Keep."

Mina's face flushed with warmth at the memory. He'd left her breathless and confused that night, and then she had used her newfound status to have Lord Klodian send him to the Dracan Dominion. It all seemed so long ago, and yet, standing with him now, it felt as though he'd only been gone a few days.

"You don't have to apologize for that," Mina

said. "It was nice."

They stared at each other in silence for a moment, and Caden drew close and placed a hand on her neck, rubbing his thumb along her cheek. Her heart began racing, and she leaned toward him. He met her, their lips pressing together. Fire coursed through her, burning under her skin. It gave her desires she never knew she wanted. When Caden broke away from her, it was like waking from a dream.

"I'm glad you weren't upset with our first kiss. I must admit, the fear that you hated me for it has kept me awake many nights. After Thais betrayed me to Captain Eduard and had me sent out here, I thought I'd never see you again."

"What do you mean? What did Thais tell Captain Eduard?"

"I found something in the ruins of Slia, a stone. I didn't know it at the time, but it's a piece of armor that Lord D'Lance's men used to protect them from dragon fire. Lord D'Lance destroyed that city with his dragon riders. Thais wanted me to tell Captain Eduard what I had found, but I refused. The next thing I knew, I was being locked up in the dungeon."

Mina could feel her throat constricting. He thought Thais was responsible for his departure from the Thophate? "Did Thais tell you she said something?"

"No, but she must have. There's no other explanation for why I was sent here."

"I thought you wanted to earn fame and riches? Didn't you say you wanted to transfer to a Dominion where you could go into battle and make a name for yourself?"

"I did, but after I met you and Thais, I changed my mind. I'll meet her on the battlefield one day, and only one of us is going to walk off of it alive."

"Caden, there's something I need to tell you," Mina said, her tone lowering.

"What is it?"

"Thais isn't the one who got you sent out here. It was me."

Caden frowned, his brow creasing.

"I'm sorry. I thought it was what you wanted. After I saved Lord Klodian's life out in the mesas, he asked me how he could repay me. I asked him to transfer you to a Dominion where you would get time on the battlefield. You were transferred because of me."

The look on his face made her stomach drop. She knew what he must be thinking. He probably hated her now and regretted ever kissing her in the first place.

"I'm a fool," he whispered. "All this time, I thought …" His eyes met hers, and she felt as if he was searching her soul somehow.

"I'm sorry," she repeated.

"Don't be. I'm not mad at you, just … surprised. I had no idea. Thank the gods that Thais doesn't know the things I've said about her beneath my breath since then. She'd want to pummel me for sure."

Relief washed over Mina like a soothing wave of cool water.

"Thank you for not being mad. I thought I was doing the most unselfish thing because I didn't want you to leave."

"Things could have gone better, but it seems to have all worked out. We're both here now, and we both have dragon companions."

"Except yours is a murderous lunatic," Mina said.

"You don't know her as I do. She hasn't murdered anyone."

"Yet."

"Our forces should ally against Lord D'Lance. We're stronger together. I know they have a turbulent past, but uniting against a common enemy for the greater good is hard to argue with. This might be the best way for the dragons to mend their differences."

"I don't think the Enclave would agree. What Lireth did was unforgivable, even after all this time. If there is truly a bond between you two, you know her thoughts. She isn't simply misguided, she's evil. The Enclave will never ally with her, and she's made her feelings clear. She plans to go after them once Lord D'Lance is dead."

"She has said the same thing to me," Caden replied. "Perhaps the Enclave deserves to fall."

Mina pulled away from him, scowling.

"You don't know what you're saying. I've seen the Enclave. They want what's best for their kind. Lireth wants only death and destruction. Surely you see the problem with that?"

"New things will rise from the ashes. It is the way of life."

"You've changed," Mina said, backing away further. "Our destinies may be entwined, but they are not united."

Caden stared at her in silence. She silently prayed that he would see reason and make the right choice. His facial expression turned to one of anger.

"You are the one who has changed. You think to lecture me? Only one person standing here is responsible for the death of dragons, and it isn't me. I can see why Lireth hates your dragons. They have allied themselves with a murderer."

His words stung her deeply. She could feel Gedrith's presence in her mind and allowed his strength to flow through her. Mina steeled her emotions.

"Leave," she said.

They stared death at one another until Caden snorted and stormed off. She watched him go, and he didn't look back once.

It was the second time she watched him leave as

her heart broke.

8

Caden stomped through the undergrowth, fuming with anger. He couldn't believe that Mina had refused to ally with him. She thought he had changed, but she was wrong. Or if he had, it was only that he wasn't blind anymore. He had purpose, *real* purpose. Fame and fortune were the things he wanted before, but now he wanted to ensure Lireth succeeded in every endeavor.

He reached the camp and went straight to her usual spot. She was there waiting for him.

"Are you all right?" he asked. "I tried to help you, but there's not much I can do against a dragon."

I am fine, but I see you aren't. What happened? Anger radiates from you like the sun.

He debated not telling her, but he knew she would probe his mind and find out, regardless.

"The girl with the dragons … her name is Mina. I know her from the Thophate Dominion. She said she is bonded to the red dragon." Caden was still curious about the bond, but he wasn't sure how to broach the subject.

I am familiar with Gedrith. We have much history together. It's a shame that he's given his loyalty to the Enclave.

"So has Mina. I offered her a place among our

forces, and she refused."

The Enclave has a way of distorting the innocent and making them into zealots of their cause. Once I burn their world to ash, their slaves will be free to think for themselves. I can sense your feelings for the girl are strong. You mustn't let your emotions cloud your judgement. There may come a day when you must kill her.

Caden was angry with her, true, but that didn't mean he wanted her dead. He was mostly convinced that she would come around, he just didn't know if the red dragon would hinder that.

Will you be able to kill her if it comes to that?

"I don't know."

Then I will make it easy for you. You are to kill her if you see her again, Lireth said. *That is my decree.*

Caden knelt before her and bowed his head. He kept his mind clear so that she couldn't discern his true feelings about the order.

"As you command," he said.

Good. Your loyalty is stronger than that of my brethren. You've done something very few have done before. You've impressed me.

"I am honored to do so. Are we safe here, or should we move the camp again?"

We will stay where we are. If Gedrith thinks to intimidate me, he is wrong. I do not fear him. It is he who should fear me.

"Should we take the fight to them? I can gather our forces and lead them there under the cover of night."

No, Lireth growled. *I need more of my brethren at my side first. Lord D'Lance is your only concern for now. We will deal with Gedrith after Lord D'Lance has fallen. I am leaving and will return tonight.*

"Is there anything you want done while you are away?"

Must I instruct you in everything?

"No, of course not."

Good.

Lireth stretched her wings out and took to the air, flying north. Caden watched until she was no longer visible, then he returned to the camp and found Bast.

"I need a few scouts," he said. "Two or three draman at the most. They need to be stealthy."

"Is this for something the master wants?"

"No, it's something for me."

Bast nodded. "What is the task?"

"I need them to keep an eye on someone."

"The girl?"

"Yes."

"Very well. I'll post them at the cave. If she goes anywhere, you'll know."

"Thank you, my friend. Did we get the rest of the provisions from the raid earlier?"

"Yes," Bast replied. "We have enough rice and grain to last us a week, maybe longer. It helps, but we still need more supplies."

"If Lireth gets her brethren to join her, then we'll have all we need when Velbridge burns. I hope she will give us a rest before marching us to the desert."

"The desert?"

"I forgot to tell you. Lireth wants to attack the home of the metallic dragons after we've dealt with Lord D'Lance."

Bast's left eye twitched, but he said nothing.

"Is that a problem?"

"No, but we will need many things for a journey that long. And what of the other Dominions? We may find trouble waiting for us, especially as word travels. And if word has not reached the other Dominions, what will the other lords think of an army marching through their territory? There is much to consider."

"I agree," Caden replied. "We'll need to start planning soon. If Lireth has her way, we'll be marching to the Long Sands before the embers of Velbridge have cooled. I'm going for a walk. Let me know when the scouts have something."

"As you command," Bast replied.

Caden left the camp and wandered through the

woods on his own, trying to clear his mind. Mina had him wound up with anger and frustration. Now that Lireth had ordered him to kill her … he mentally felt along his mind to see if she was present. Her presence was there, but it was faint.

Good, he thought. He rarely had time for his own thoughts, and while he didn't normally mind the lack of privacy, he had tumultuous feelings about her new orders. Could he really kill Mina? Of course he *could,* but *would* he? Did he have the conviction to? Caden was glad Lireth was away. If she knew that he had doubts about her command, she'd be furious.

And what of Bast? His reaction to the news that they would march to the desert to battle the Enclave didn't bode well. Were the draman as loyal as Lireth assumed they were? Bast had once said that the humanity in him battled against the dragon. Perhaps they all suffered from that internal battle. And if they did … well, who knew what would happen if the human part won.

If the draman rebelled against Lord D'Lance, there was nothing to keep them from breaking ranks with Lireth. They revered her as though she were a goddess. While he admitted she was awe-inspiring and intimidating, she was mortal just like he was. She was no goddess, no matter how the draman worshipped her.

"Stop it," Caden muttered to himself. His thoughts were straying too far for comfort. Perhaps it was a good thing that Lireth stayed in his mind so much. He couldn't be trusted otherwise. It seemed he had an internal battle going on as well. He'd never doubted his master before. Why was he doing it now? The answer was obvious.

It was Mina.

She was the reason he'd been sent away from the Thophate. She was also the reason for everything he'd been through. If he'd remained under Lord Klodian's command, none of the terrible things that had befallen him would have happened. Yes, the blame resided with her. She was reckless and untrustworthy. Perhaps Lireth was right. She wasn't clouded with bias, after all.

Mina had to die.

9

Mina sat in the cave's entrance in front of a small fire, staring off as her thoughts led her on a wild ride, her dinner long since cold. She wasn't the only one bonded to a dragon now. The thought didn't sit well with her, but only because Caden's dragon was evil. The thing that bothered her the most was that he'd tried to convince her to join the wrong side.

Was it her fault? She had been the one to get Lord Klodian to send him away, after all. Yet, while that was true, she didn't control his thoughts and actions. He had chosen to follow Lireth, to align himself with darkness. No, she decided, it was not her fault. Gedrith told her that Lireth was deceptive, and Mina was convinced that the dragon had bonded with Caden without his knowledge.

I believe you are correct in that line of thinking, Gedrith's voice entered her thoughts. *He may not even be aware that she's influencing his thoughts.*

Mina sighed and tossed her food into the fire, then rose to her feet. Her appetite was gone. She put the fire out and walked further into the cave. It was dark for a few feet, but glowing moss spider-webbed across the ceiling of the cave, giving the impression that the stone was cracked.

It doesn't seem fair that Caden doesn't know what she's doing to him, she said, sitting beside

Gedrith.

Life is rarely fair.

I know that more than anyone. My point is that I don't think it's fair that a dragon can have so much power over another being.

It is the natural order of things. Some species are more powerful than others.

Mina leaned her back against Gedrith and stared up at the glowing moss. If she was going to kill Lord D'Lance, then she needed to familiarize herself with the layout of Velbridge and, if possible, find a way into the castle.

What do we do about Lireth? She asked. *She may disrupt our plans.*

I will deal with her myself, but I must wait for the right opportunity. In the meantime, my brethren are going to give Lord D'Lance a few headaches. They plan to attack some of his outposts on the border. Since he's using his draman and dragon riders to patrol the area near the castle, it is the safest option to avoid an open battle.

Good idea. Mina stifled a yawn, her exhaustion much stronger than she realized.

Sleep while you can, Gedrith said. *Soon we will not have time to rest.*

Mina had a feeling he was right. She fell asleep, and the next thing she knew, slanted rays of sunlight were shining into the cave. Gedrith was still asleep, so she quietly rose to her feet and slipped out of the cave, casting a backward glance over her shoulder. Rubbing the sleep from her eyes, she stretched and surveyed the forest. Birds were chirping overhead, so she knew there weren't any draman nearby. At least, she hoped not.

Her dreams had fueled an idea, and she wanted to carry it out before Gedrith knew what she was doing. Her stomach was empty, but she didn't have time for breakfast. Velbridge was calling her name.

Mina turned northwest and began the trek to Lord D'Lance's city. If she was going to kill the Dominion Lord, then she needed to know the layout of his domain, and she figured it would be easier to do alone. It wasn't like Gedrith could go with her, anyway. The sight of a dragon flying toward the city wouldn't just cause a panic, but it would draw Lord D'Lance's attention. The longer she could keep the element of surprise, the better her chances of success.

The woods soon gave way to open flatlands, and in the distance, Mina spotted the walls of Velbridge. With the city in view, she quickened her pace. By the time she reached the gates, droplets of sweat had collected on her forehead. A multitude of guards were keeping a watchful eye on everyone coming and going through the gates, but otherwise, they didn't harass anyone. Mina held her breath as she passed them, praying to Avera that they wouldn't stop her.

Relief washed over her and she relaxed a little once she was inside the city. Patrols were everywhere, composed of both humans and draman.

It surprised her to see the creatures walking about freely, and the city folk shied away from them whenever they approached. The tenseness in the air was obvious, and Mina couldn't help but wonder what had caused it.

She wandered along the main road before turning down a side street and entering a tavern. The place had a light crowd, and Mina took a seat at the bar.

A plump, bald man rushed over and smiled warmly.

"What can I get you?" he asked.

"What kind of food do you have?"

"The usual fare. How does eggs and sausage sound?"

"That sounds delicious."

"Perfect! And an ale to wash it down with?"

"Do you have water?"

The man laughed. "We do, but we don't get many requests for it. I'll have it to you shortly."

Mina watched him bustle away and glanced around the room. Most of the patrons were drinking ale, and she couldn't believe they were partaking of it so early in the day. At the nearest table, a group of men were talking about the increased patrols within the city. Mina pretended to mind her own business, but she listened intently to their conversation.

"All these creatures are bad for business," one of them said. "Everyone's afraid to leave their homes, and I can't sell anything if I don't have any customers."

Another man nodded. "My business has dried up completely within a matter of days. I don't know about you, but I blame whoever was behind that failed attack. Lord D'Lance may have had those foul beasts this entire time, but I'd rather he kept them a secret."

"I hate to admit it, but I might have to pack up and move somewhere else if things don't change quickly. I've got a family to feed."

Mina frowned. A failed attack? She wondered if it had to do with Caden. The clatter of a plate made her turn around and she saw the barkeep had delivered her food along with a wooden mug filled with clear liquid.

"That'll be two silvers."

Mina reached down at her waist and realized she didn't have any money. The look on her face must have given the barkeep a clue because he smiled again.

"First time customer?"

She nodded.

"It's on the house, but next time, you'll have to pay."

"Thank you, but I can't accept—"

"You can and you will," he replied. "Enjoy!"

He rushed away to another customer before she could argue any further. She stared at the plate of steaming eggs and considered leaving, but hunger won over and she devoured them ravenously. The water was cool and quenched her thirst.

Where are you? Gedrith's voice startled her.

Velbridge. I wanted to learn the layout of the city.

Did you see the draman?

Yes. The city is crawling with them. There was an attack recently, and Lord D'Lance has heightened security everywhere.

Not those draman. The ones that were in the woods.

Mina's brow creased. *What do you mean?*

You're being followed.

10

Caden was up before the sun rose. The sound of flapping wings had woken him. Not that he'd been in a deep sleep, anyway. His dreams had been dark and kept him from being able to rest. He stretched his muscles and trekked across the camp, heading to Lireth's usual spot.

It surprised him to see that she had returned with more than a few dragons. There were a dozen of the creatures, most of them as ebon scaled as she was, but there were four exceptions. Two green dragons, a blue, and a white. The green ones were thick and bulky, but they weren't as large as Lireth. The white one was the smallest of them all but looked just as fierce. Of them all, the blue one caught his attention the most.

It was the largest of the newcomers, dwarfing the green duo. Many of the scales on its face were chipped or missing completely, giving the dragon an ominous appearance. Where entire scales were absent, the flesh was scarred and mottled. He tore his gaze away before the beast looked at him.

"I see you were successful," Caden said to Lireth.

Their numbers are less than I wanted, but I will take them. More will come when they see the devastation I unleash upon Lord D'Lance's domain.

"They will certainly bolster our forces, but he

will know we are coming long before we reach the castle. A dozen dragons in the sky would be hard to miss."

That is why we will take down his scouts.

"The draman can manage that, but they'll need to find a way to sneak into the city. The place has guards everywhere. We can send them ahead of us, but their task will be a challenge."

I am speaking of the dragons that patrol the skies. There are only a few. With them out of the way, he will be defenseless against our onslaught.

"You are as clever as you are awe-inspiring," Caden complimented.

You speak the obvious. Inform Bast that he is in command until you return.

"Return from where?"

You and I will be the ones to take down the scouts.

"What good will I do? I can't injure a dragon, nor could I attack one from the ground even if I could."

You will ride on my back. Lireth snorted derisively. Tendrils of smoke drifted out of her nostrils. *Use your brain before I find another use for you.*

Caden bowed to her. "My apologies," he said. "I didn't realize you were going to grant me the honor."

It is a privilege I give you for being joined to

me.

"Is that the same as being bonded? Mina mentioned being bonded to Gedrith. Do you and I share the same connection?"

Lireth regarded him in silence for a moment.

Yes, but our bond is different. When I feel you are ready, I will teach you about it.

"I look forward to proving myself worthy in your eyes."

Caden returned to the camp and found Bast eating breakfast. He was sitting beside the glowing embers of a fire from the night before. Their eyes met, and the draman rose to his feet.

"What is it?"

"You're in command while I'm gone. I'm going with our master to clear the skies of enemies."

"How many men do you need?"

"None," Caden replied. "It's just the master and me. Her orders, not mine."

He could tell by Bast's scowl that the draman didn't approve.

"Keep the men here in the camp except for the scouts. They need to be prepared for battle. I have a feeling that when we return, she'll want to attack Velbridge."

Bast's expression brightened.

"We're still vastly outnumbered, but the men will be ready."

"That shouldn't be a problem. Some of our master's allies have joined her."

"We may yet have our revenge," Bast said.

"Indeed. Any word from the draman in the woods?"

Bast looked past Caden, toward Lireth.

"Nothing yet, but I've instructed them to report in every twelve hours. I should have something for you when you get back."

"Good. She wants to kill Lord D'Lance as much as any of us, but I doubt she'll get near the castle gates before she's caught. She's not a soldier, so I don't understand why she thinks she'll be successful."

"There's no telling. Perhaps she has a sickness of the mind. It can make people do strange things."

"I can only hope that's true. I'll return as soon as possible."

Caden went to his tent and slipped a chainmail shirt on. He didn't want to be weighed down too heavily, especially if things went bad and he was forced to escape on his own. He also belted on his sword, though he didn't know why he bothered. It wasn't like he could strike down a dragon with one.

He stopped by the chef's tent and grabbed some cheese and rice, scarfing it down as he walked back to Lireth's position. She was with her brethren, and they were all gathered in a circle. Caden waited nearby, taking in the details of the other black dragons. Lireth was longer and larger than all of them. He suspected that had something to do with her age, but that was only an assumption. The dragons broke away from each other, and Lireth looked at him.

Come. The blood of our enemies shall rain upon the ground.

Caden climbed onto her back, feeling overwhelmed and unworthy. He sat between her shoulders and grabbed onto the scales of her neck. She stretched her wings out and took to the sky, the wind buffeting him violently. He held on as tightly as he could, but he was no match for the forces of nature. He lost his grip and whipped back, crashing against Lireth's back and knocking his head.

Your grip is too weak. If you can't hold on, you'll fall to your death.

Her dire words gave him the push he needed to force himself up, and he grabbed hold of her scales again. He found it helped to lean low, practically hugging her. The wind still battered him, but it was no longer threatening to send him tumbling off her back. It wasn't long into their flight before Caden heard a roaring sound ahead. He lifted his head and blinked rapidly, trying to keep his eyes from being ripped out of their sockets.

A dragon was coming toward them. He wasn't sure, but it looked like someone was standing on its back. Lireth bellowed and angled herself into its path. If Caden hadn't emptied his bladder earlier, he was certain he would have pissed on himself now.

He could see the ground below, but something about not having his feet firmly planted on it made his stomach queasy.

He watched helplessly as the dragon steadily got closer. Once it was almost upon them, Lireth barrel rolled to the right, forcing a scream from his lips. His arms and legs felt like they were slipping, and just as he thought he was going to fall, Lireth leveled out and breathed a fiery torrent at their enemy as they passed one another.

The flames streamed over the other dragon harmlessly, but the rider on its back screamed as they overcame him. The fire sizzled from existence, and Caden saw there was nothing left of the person. Lireth wheeled around and went after the dragon. She extended her forelegs and flexed her claws wide. As she dropped, Caden held his breath.

11

Why would they be following me? Mina asked.

I'm sure they are associated with your friend.

He's not my friend. Not anymore.

It stung her to admit that. Caden had been the first and only person to befriend her despite her deformity. To see him walking toward destruction beside Lireth was heart-wrenching, but she'd tried to dissuade him from the path. She had done her part. The decision to turn away from evil was his alone.

Mina's hand drifted to the hilt of her blade, and she scanned the room. Two draman were sitting at a table by the door. She hadn't noticed them before, but she wasn't paying much attention to the surrounding people, either.

You need to be more alert, Gedrith said.

I was just thinking the same thing. No one other than Caden knows who I am, and I wasn't expecting him to keep eyes on me.

You should come back to the cave. They won't dare try anything with me and my brethren beside you.

I have something else in mind. If Caden thinks he's the only one with things up his sleeves, he's about to be surprised.

Mina left the tavern and headed toward the castle, keeping a brisk pace. As she turned onto another street, she casually looked behind her and spotted the two draman from the tavern. Gedrith was right, she *was* being followed. The creatures kept their distance, and Mina decided she wasn't in danger.

She reached the walls that separated the castle from the city and wandered along the perimeter, looking for a stealthy way across. Heavily armed guards were posted every few feet, and they eyed her distrustfully as she walked.

Lord D'Lance has the castle protected like it's full of treasure, she told Gedrith.

He holds dragons and eggs captive. Those are more valuable than gold and gems. Both give him more power than money could ever buy.

I suppose you're right. He may not be afraid to let the world see his dragons and draman, but he's clearly afraid of losing the ones he hasn't converted to his cause.

They haven't been converted, Gedrith said. *They are bonded against their will. Whether they are locked in the castle or not, they are prisoners.*

Mina walked the entire length of the wall and turned down an alley. It was a dead-end, taking her to a wall too high to climb. A pile of trash was the only place to hide, and she grimaced as she hurriedly hid among the filth. She pinched her nose and waited.

A few moments later, the two draman stepped into view. It confused them when they didn't see her and they began talking to one another in another language. Mina held completely still, breathing as softly as she dared. The draman began arguing and then stormed out of the alley, turning to the right. Mina waited a moment longer before climbing out of the garbage. She ran to the end of the alley and peeked around the corner. The draman were still arguing.

She followed after them, ducking into doorways or blending in with crowds to keep them from seeing her. They returned to the tavern from earlier, and Mina looked for the nearest human guards. A group of them were marching along the street, and she intercepted them.

"Oh, thank Avera you're here! There are two of those creatures in the tavern."

"The draman are official guards in Lord D'Lance's army," one of them said dismissively, but the look on his face told Mina that he wasn't happy about it.

"They aren't Lord D'Lance's men, sir. They're defectors."

That caught the attention of all the soldiers.

"How do you know?"

"I overheard them plotting to hurt Lord D'Lance."

"You said there were two of them?"

"Yes, sir. They're armed with swords, too."

The man looked at his fellows and nodded toward the tavern. They broke formation and headed for the building.

"We'll take care of them," the soldier said.

Mina watched them converge on the place and storm inside. A commotion erupted within, and the two draman were escorted out forcefully. They were bound with shackles and the soldiers marched them toward the castle. Mina smiled. She could play Caden's game all day, and she would win. He might have an army with him, but he couldn't openly march them after her. He was stuck in the shadows while she could walk freely.

That was clever, Gedrith chuckled.

I learned many things while serving Lord Klodian, one of which was how to be petty. Caden doesn't know what he's getting himself into.

Be careful that the taste of hatred does not blind you. Some lines can never be uncrossed.

I'm not blind, she replied. *I'm teaching him a lesson. Just because he's gained power doesn't mean he can do with it as he pleases.*

Lireth will drive him into madness. She may already be doing so. It wouldn't surprise me if he tries to kill you.

Mina frowned. She wanted nothing to do with Caden, but that didn't mean she wanted him to die. If Lireth twisted his mind into making him try to kill her, would she be able to stop him? And if not, did she have the strength to kill him first? She wasn't so sure.

Hopefully, it won't come to that, she said.

Unless he leaves her, a battle between you two is inevitable. You are the champion of the Enclave, and he is hers. Once Lord D'Lance is dead, I do not doubt that there will be war among the dragons.

As long as that war doesn't spill over onto humanity, then let them fight.

There is no 'them' anymore. If there is war, you will be involved.

Mina didn't like the idea of being in the middle of a war with men, let alone one with dragons. If Caden didn't change his mind and find a way to sever his connection to Lireth, then deep down she knew they would end up in battle against one another.

And that scared her more than anything.

12

Caden clenched his jaw against the fear welling within him. Lireth crashed onto the enemy, her claws scraping against the dragon's scales. Raw anger filled Caden's mind, and he knew it was coming from Lireth. Her rage was overwhelming and it made him dizzy. He tightened his grip on her and tried to put up a mental block.

Fire. Death. Fury.

Images and emotions swirled chaotically before his eyes, real and yet imagined. A distant memory flashed briefly, a scene of dragons battling one another. Just as quickly as it entered his mind, it was gone, leaving him reeling.

Smoke. Bodies. Desolation.

Caden used all of his mental facilities to push the images away. With his mind clear, he saw Lireth had the other dragon at her mercy. With a mighty swipe, she tore through the dragon's wing membrane with her talons. The beast issued a roar of pain and plummeted toward the ground. Caden averted his eyes.

Traitors are sentenced to death.

Even if they are forced? Caden posed the question without knowing if Lireth would hear him.

You've learned to mind-speak on your own. I'm impressed. Regardless of whether Lord D'Lance has forced the bond or not, they are tainted by him and cannot be trusted. They are not fit to join us until he is dead.

When he dies, will the bonds be destroyed?

Yes. His magic will die with him.

Good.

There are a few more dragons on patrol to remove, and then we launch our attack.

Caden stiffened. *We're not ready. Our draman are still outnumbered, not to mention that we don't have enough supplies.*

My brethren and I will do most of the work. You and the draman will enter the city after we've ravaged it. You will concentrate your effort on the soldiers first, then the rest can be killed.

The rest?

Anyone living under Lord D'Lance's banner is subject to his punishment as well.

But ... what if they are innocent?

No human is innocent. This shall be a lasting lesson for anyone who thinks to harm and control dragons.

Caden's face creased with concern. How could she ask him to kill innocent people? In the back of his mind, a memory came to the forefront. The night he'd killed Lord D'Lance's potential assassin. If he'd known then what he knew now, he would have let the man live. Lord D'Lance was wicked and deserved his fate, but the people who lived in

Velbridge were innocent, weren't they?

Perhaps not. Perhaps they were just as wicked as their lord, but they were better at hiding their atrocities. Even he had dark thoughts at times. He didn't act on them, but that didn't mean other people refrained. He supposed Lireth was right. These people needed to be punished. Obliterating the city would be a harsh lesson, but one that would never be forgotten.

Very well, Caden said. *Our forces will be ready at your command.*

I knew my trust was well placed in you.

Lireth wheeled to the west and sped over the landscape. Caden held on tightly, excitement brimming within him. All his life he'd wanted to show others that they didn't have to be a tyrant to have fame and riches, and now he was about to prove it. He would help Lireth wipe the evil from the Dracan Dominion, and the people would rejoice.

And if they didn't, then they too would be destroyed.

The next patrol they encountered was completely unprepared for Lireth's fury. He'd thought the lone dragon before had been easy prey for his master, but she proved that creature's death had been merciful in comparison. The patrol was a trio of dragons with riders, and they fell to her flames and claws with a violence he'd never witnessed before. When their bodies fell from the sky and struck the ground, she swooped down and tore their lifeless forms limb from limb.

Caden reveled in the power of his master. No one could stop her. She would have her revenge on Lord D'Lance, on the Enclave … the world would burn, just as she said. When they returned to the camp, they were both covered in blood.

Prepare the draman. Once the city is on fire and the castle falls, send them in.

As you command, Caden replied.

He strode through the camp shouting for Bast. The draman rushed into view.

"What is it? Are you all right?" He skidded to a stop and sniffed the air. "That's dragon blood." Bast looked past him to where Lireth normally stayed.

"All is well, my friend. Lireth has cleared the patrols from the sky in preparation for our attack. Gather the men. We're going to war."

"Now?"

"Yes. Once Lireth destroys the castle, we will sweep the city and deal with the others."

Bast hesitated, but he nodded, his reptilian pupils turning to thin slits. "I trust that she will lead us to victory."

"For her glory," Caden replied.

He left Bast and headed for the stream in the woods. The stench of the dragon blood was making his stomach queasy. He didn't bother taking off his armor as he marched into the water and began washing the blood off.

Cupping his hands, he brought some of the cold

water to his face, sucking in a sharp breath as it splashed onto his skin. He removed most of the grime, but he didn't bother deep cleaning the armor. They would soon spill more blood, and he didn't want to waste his efforts. When he stepped out of the stream, Bast was waiting for him.

"We don't have enough men," the draman said.

"I know, but our master and the other dragons will reduce most of the city's defenses, so we won't have much to contend with. If Lord D'Lance's soldiers haven't fled by the time we arrive, they're either fools or insane."

Caden wiped the water from his eyes and face and looked at Bast directly. Judging by his demeanor, he could tell Bast was uneasy.

"If I wasn't confident in this, I wouldn't be asking this of you, or of them. Lireth can't be stopped by anything Lord D'Lance has in his employ."

"I was hoping more of my brethren would have joined us. Killing my own kind feels … immoral. Anyone under the influence of Lord D'Lance's magic will stay and fight as long as he's alive."

"I understand your reservations. I have my own, but this is the right path. Once that tyrant is dead, the world will be better off. If it were easy to stand up to injustice, everyone would do it."

Bast sighed. "I know you wouldn't lead us astray, but the human in me has doubts. I will trust our master's plan. If all goes well, we will finally have some peace."

"This is only the first step toward peace. The Enclave will fall next."

"And what about after that?"

Caden shrugged. "We will go where Lireth wants and do as she commands."

Bast bowed his head and left in silence. He may not have said anything, but Caden recognized the draman's conflict. It wasn't much different from his own, but whereas his bond with Lireth gave him the strength and wisdom to see past the doubts, Bast did not.

Perhaps the draman had outlived his usefulness.

13

Mina spent a few hours watching the castle gates, and she could now determine a definitive rotation of shifts among the guards. They changed out every hour, but as they made the switch, those being replaced waited until they were relieved. It was precise, leaving her with no opportunity to get into the castle grounds.

By the time Mina felt hungry, she realized it was already past noon. With no money to buy food, she decided to return to the cave and see if she could scrounge something up. As she navigated the streets, she noticed people were looking at the sky and pointing. She slowed her pace and glanced up. At first, she saw nothing other than a few sparse clouds.

"Are those Lord D'Lance's sky patrols?" someone asked.

Mina squinted and made out about a dozen splotches that steadily grew larger. Had the Enclave sent more dragons to harass Lord D'Lance? The crowd of people stopping to stare continued to swell, and they speculated what the shapes were. As the seconds turned to minutes, the truth became clear.

Mina's stomach churned, but it wasn't from hunger. The unknown shapes were dragons, but they weren't metallic like Gedrith and his brethren.

They were chromatic dragons. And the one leading them was the black behemoth bonded to Caden. Mina's mind screamed at her to run, but her legs froze in place. The dragon fear was thick in the air, and she watched helplessly as the dragons descended on Velbridge.

They roared, their battle cries so loud that she thought she would go deaf. Lireth passed over the crowd of people and unleashed her fire. The flames bathed the buildings along the street, setting them ablaze. The heat singed her hair and burned her flesh. A scream pierced the air, and Mina felt sorry for the person before she realized it was her own.

Where are you? Gedrith's voice cut through the fear and she slumped to her knees.

I'm still in Velbridge. Lireth just attacked!

I'm coming to get you.

No! Even with your brethren, we are outnumbered. I'll try to get out of the city.

How many are with her?

Mina gingerly looked skyward and saw numerous black dragons, a couple of green ones, as well as a blue and a white.

Over a dozen, she said.

She has found allies, then. The city will be destroyed by the time the Enclave can send help. It is up to me and my brethren.

She'll kill you.

If I die protecting you, then I have done my duty.

Get near the walls if you can't escape the city. I'm on my way.

Mina didn't bother arguing with him. She struggled to her feet and began jogging along the street, heading south toward the main gates. Thick smoke filled the air, burning her eyes and lungs. She coughed and buried her mouth in the crook of her elbow, trying not to breathe it in. The heat coming off the burning buildings drove her to turn down a side street, and she tripped over a prone body.

She fell, smashing the side of her face hard on the cobbled stones. The body she stumbled over was a woman, and a small child, a girl, was sitting nearby, tears streaming down her face. The girl was crying and moving her mouth, but Mina could barely hear her. She offered a quick prayer to Avera that she wasn't truly deaf now and crawled over to the child.

"Come with me," she said, not sure if she was yelling or not. She held her hands out and the child latched onto her. Mina held her close and got up, continuing her trek through the burning city. She passed more bodies, most of them charred, and eventually found her way back to the principal thoroughfare.

Small groups of people had gathered and they were trying to battle the flames, but Mina thought their pursuit was hopeless. Unless Lireth and the others were driven away, nothing would be left after their rampage.

A grizzled old man was gathering the more helpless to him, and Mina diverted her steps to him and handed over the child. She couldn't take care of the girl, even if she wanted to. With the child as safe as possible, she sprinted for the main gates. An inordinate amount of people fleeing the devastation blocked the way out, and they were all pushing and shoving against one another.

I'm near the gates, but I can't get out, Mina said.

The smoke overhead swirled and cleared away to reveal Gedrith. He landed atop the wall, his rear claws snapping onto the stone to keep him balanced. His head swiveled back and forth, enormous eyes scanning the sky over the city.

Mina spotted stairs leading to the top of the wall and ran to them, taking them two at a time. She hastily climbed onto Gedrith's back and looked out over Velbridge. A haze of smoke hid most of the cityscape, but she could clearly see Lireth and her minions flaming more parts of the city. The flames had yet to reach the castle, though.

We need to get help.

There isn't time, Gedrith replied.

Is there no way to get word to the Enclave?

I can send one of my silver brethren, but even with their speed, it will be too late before help arrives. Most of the city burns even now.

I'm less concerned with the city and more worried about the people, not to mention Lord

D'Lance. Why hasn't he come out to fight Lireth? Where are his dragons?

Perhaps he doesn't have as many as we thought.

As if to reject that statement, a horn blared in the distance. A moment later, more dragons filled the air and a battle erupted.

We should help the people get to safety, Mina said.

No, we should join the fight. If my brethren and I are lucky, we can kill Lord D'Lance and Lireth at the same time.

Mina looked from the dragons to the city. She didn't know what to do. Either option held its own risks, but she didn't see how she could truly help against the other dragons.

You are my rider, and your place with me, Gedrith said. *You must stop doubting yourself and learn to trust me.*

He was right. She knew that, but she still had her reservations.

Fine, she replied. *Let's end this.*

She drew her sword and he leaped into the air, the wind from his wings pushing the smoke in all directions. Here and there she glimpsed ravaged sections of the city. It broke her heart to see so many bodies littering the streets. The three silver dragons that the Enclave had sent joined them, forming an arrow formation in front of them.

My brethren will target Lord D'Lance.

What about us?

We will deal with Lireth.

As they closed the distance to the battle, Mina saw Caden wasn't with Lireth. In fact, none of the Lireth's dragons had riders.

Wait. Something's off.

What is it?

If Caden's not with Lireth, where is he?

She scanned the ground and found her answer. He was on the ground, leading a force of draman to the city.

14

Caden stood with Bast in front of their force of draman, watching Lireth and her brethren wreak destruction on Velbridge. Flames peaked over the walls, and billowing smoke drifted into the sky above the city, creating a massive gray cloud.

"Now?" Bast asked.

"Not yet."

He was waiting on Lireth to give the command, but it worried him that she was too caught up in her emotions. Violent joy filled his mind through their bond, and his skin tingled from the sheer power she displayed. Torrents of fire left her maw, incinerating everything below her, including portions of the stone wall.

"Our master will leave nothing standing," Bast said. "This place will be a sign of her vengeance for ages to come."

Caden didn't doubt that, but he did doubt Bast's loyalty, especially after their last conversation. He side-eyed the draman as he considered how to deal with him. Many of their forces would likely perish in the city, and he could use that as justification for Bast's absence. Lireth was so enveloped in her revenge that he doubted she was reading his thoughts.

"It's time," Caden said loudly. "To the city!"

A cheer rang from the draman behind him, and they began their trek toward Velbridge. Caden marched quickly, leading the charge to the walls. A wave of heat hit him before he was a hundred feet away. He halted and staggered back, but the draman continued, unfazed by the drastic temperature. Bast urged his fellows onward, but he stayed by Caden.

"Are you all right?"

"The heat is a bit much for me."

"I thought your armor protected from the heat of dragon fire?"

Caden watched the draman continue ahead of them, oblivious to the fact that their leaders were now at the rear. He grabbed the hilt of his sword and hesitated. What if Bast wasn't disloyal? What if Caden had misjudged the draman's words? If that was the case, killing him would be wrong.

And yet ... if he was right, he'd be protecting Lireth and stopping dissension before it could spread to the others.

"What is it?" Bast stared him in the eyes.

"I'm sorry, friend."

Caden drew his blade and jabbed forward, aiming the tip of the sword for the vulnerable fleshy spot of the draman's neck that was unprotected by armor. Bast moved with a quickness that surprised him, and the draman brought his own blade up, knocking Caden's strike to the side with a clang.

"What are you doing?" he hissed.

"You've lost your trust in our master," Caden replied, circling to the left. Bast mirrored his steps to the right.

"I swore an oath to her. I would never go back on my word."

"How do I know that? You question her decision to march to The Long Sands. If you were loyal to her, you wouldn't have."

"Bah! You're blinded by something, but I don't know what it is. Just because I question something doesn't mean I have forsaken my oath. Lireth rescued me. She rescued all of us."

"She saved me from death," Caden said. "I see more clearly than you, it seems. I would never question her."

"We are marching to victory, and you attack me for nothing. Please, let us call peace and battle together as brothers in arms."

Caden knew the draman was trying to trick him. He lunged ahead, jabbing with his blade. Again, Bast blocked the strike, retreating from Caden's reach instead of launching his own attack. The draman was clever, but Caden wouldn't be fooled. He went on the offensive, slashing and stabbing. Bast was his equal, if not superior, and the draman deflected every blow, backpedaling instead of fighting him.

"Fight back, you coward!"

"You are mad," Bast said, his reptilian pupils nothing more than slits. "Stop this foolishness before …”

“Before what?” Caden demanded.

“Before one of us dies untimely. Our master will not be pleased, regardless of who falls.”

“She’ll be glad to know that I have removed a traitor when you are dead.” Caden could feel his anger building. The draman was playing stupid, trying to get him to lower his guard. He refused to believe that Bast was still a loyal servant of their master. Bast looked past him, up at the sky, and his expression hardened.

“The enemy is coming!”

Caden growled and swung his sword at the draman. Bast jumped backward out of range and Caden stumbled from his momentum, but he quickly recovered. Something large and heavy hit the ground behind him, but before he could look, something struck him down. Bast turned and fled.

“Your master has killed innocent people!”

It surprised him to hear her voice. He honestly believed he’d never see her again. Or maybe it was that he hoped he wouldn’t, because that meant he would have to kill her. Caden roared in anger and got to his feet, retrieving his blade and whirling around to face her.

Mina had her sword drawn, and he could see the fury in her eyes. *Good,* he thought. It would make his task easier if she wanted to fight him.

“There are always casualties in war. Everyone

knows this."

Mina pointed toward the city. "Look at that and tell me it's not wrong."

Caden kept his gaze on her, which only seemed to infuriate her further.

"Look at it!" she screamed.

He flicked his eyes to the side briefly.

"What do you want from me, Mina? You want me to betray her? She saved my life. I am indebted to her, and I will honor her until I die."

Mina's jaw tightened and he knew that only one of them was going to walk away from this fight alive. He gripped the hilt of his sword firmly and brought the blade up.

"No!" Mina screamed. "I will kill him myself!"

Caden assumed she was talking to her dragon. The copper beast loomed behind her, his bulk just as sinuous and muscled as Lireth's. Dragon fear tugged at him, but he channeled his master's strength to push it away.

"Try if you think you can," he said.

Mina rushed him, swinging her sword wildly. She had some skill, which impressed him, but her movements showed that she was still a novice. Caden parried her strikes and stepped closer when he spotted an obvious opening in her defenses. He swiped his blade along her forearm, slicing the skin open. She cried out in pain and drew back, cursing.

Guilt assailed him. He was more practiced with

a sword than she was, and it was clear that he would win. Yet his master had ordered him to kill her if he saw her again. He was conflicted, his obligation warring with his emotions. Why did she have to be involved with Lireth's enemies?

Kill her.

Lireth was present in his mind, and her words compelled him. He attacked her ferociously, her weak attempts to block his strikes fueling his desire to see her die. Or was it his desire? It was hard to discern where he ended and Lireth began, but he supposed that was because of their bond.

Her dragon is here. If I kill her, he will kill me.

Not if I kill him first.

Lireth roared, and all eyes turned toward her approach.

15

Get down!

Mina fell to her knees and Gedrith curled his body around her, shielding her with his wings as Lireth dropped among them, spewing fire in their direction. Mina clenched her eyes closed, expecting to be burned alive. When death didn't take her, she peaked them open and saw that Gedrith's body was unharmed.

When I open my wings, get on my back as quickly as you can.

I'm ready. Mina got into a crouch and sheathed her sword.

Gedrith removed his wings from around her and she stood, risking a glance at Lireth. Caden was mounted on her back and she leaped, taking to the sky. Mina hurriedly climbed up Gedrith's shoulder and had barely seated herself before he launched into the air. They chased after Lireth, flying over the city and into the smoke.

Mina lost sight of the black dragon in the haze, but Gedrith confidently wheeled left and right, and she assumed he could see better than her. He swooped down and Lireth's tail whizzed past her head.

Hold on!

Mina gripped Gedrith's neck tightly. He angled

upward and flew higher and higher until they broke above the thick smoke that blotted out the city. Lireth was there as well, and she came straight for them.

Gedrith spread his wings out wide, catching the wind, and thrust his rear claws out to grab Lireth. She mirrored the maneuver and the two dragons locked their claws together, spinning in circles and falling toward the ground. The force of their spins was so strong that Mina lost her grip and flew backward.

Despite having fallen before, the feeling of sheer terror that enveloped her wasn't something she could ever get used to. Her stomach churned and she screamed, waving her arms frantically. As she fell, she watched Gedrith and Lireth claw and snap at one another as they continued to spiral.

Mina thought for sure that Gedrith was going to break free and come to her rescue, but that assumption was violently tossed aside when her fall was broken by the remains of a vendor cart. It collapsed under her and she gasped in surprise and agony as pain flared through every inch of her body.

She lay there unmoving for a long moment, afraid that if she tried to get up, she would discover that she'd broken some bones. Holding her breath, she sat up and was astonished to find that other than some cuts, she was unharmed. She looked up to see if the two dragons were still battling, but the smoke was thicker now than before.

I'm alive, Mina muttered as she climbed out of

the wreckage and surveyed her surroundings. She was on a street filled with vendor carts and wagons, all of them blackened and a few still burning. Distant voices echoed off the charred buildings, but she didn't see anyone in the vicinity.

Without a clear idea of what she should do, she walked toward the sound of the voices. The intense heat had subsided a little, but the smoke still choked her and burned her eyes. She blinked rapidly and turned down a side street. The voices were louder now, and she knew she was going the right way. The street widened into an open spacious square and she saw the source of the voices.

A large force of draman. They were coming out of one of the buildings, and two of them were dragging a lifeless body behind them. They stopped when they saw her, and Mina froze.

"No prisoners!" one of them yelled.

The others shouted in excitement and rushed toward her. Mina turned and bolted. She was overwhelmingly outnumbered and had no doubts that they would kill her. She zig-zagged down random streets and climbed over piles of debris in her panicked flight.

Gedrith, where are you? I need you!

She could feel his presence in her mind, but he didn't respond. He was probably still battling with Lireth. Mina skidded to a halt when she reached a bridge that spanned over a canal. The center portion of the bridge was gone, and the distance to the other side was too far for her to jump across.

Mina looked back and saw the draman were closing in on her. She cursed the creatures and jumped into the water. Her sword and chainmail weighed her down, but she kicked and swam as fast as she could, following the canal's current. The draman didn't follow her, and she floated along until she encountered a shallow spot that offered a platform for fishermen. She pulled herself out of the water and slumped onto her back, panting heavily.

A roar shattered the momentary silence and Mina sat up. It sounded like it was right above her. Something was coming.

Gedrith?

Nothing.

She got to her feet and kept her eyes on the cloud of smoke. A few moments passed, and then one of the silver dragons broke through the haze and crashed into a building. Mina gasped. His neck was twisted at an odd angle, and he was obviously dead.

Gedrith!

I'm here, he replied.

Thank Avera! Is Lireth dead?

No. Lord D'Lance joined the fight on dragon back and she went after him. Where are you?

I'm not sure. There's a canal, and one of your brethren is dead.

I saw him fall, Gedrith said sadly. *I couldn't reach him in time to help. Stay where you are.*

The sound of flapping wings signaled his approach and he descended through the smoke, landing feet first in the canal.

Are you hurt?

No, Mina answered. *Well, not seriously. I'll be bruised tomorrow, I'm sure. What about you?*

Gedrith lifted his head to reveal some damaged scales on his neck. *More battle scars.*

Where are your other brethren?

Fighting. We need to take Lireth down, but that's going to be a hard task with Lord D'Lance and his riders in the air.

Maybe he will kill Lireth and save us the trouble.

Perhaps, but it will not be easy for him. And if she falls, those allied with her will scatter. Although I despise her, her actions will help us defeat him.

Is Caden still with her?

Yes.

Mina nodded. She looked at the cut on her arm. It wasn't deep and the wound had clotted, but it still stung when she moved it. Caden had intentionally injured her, but his expression afterward had been one of remorse.

Do you think there's a way to kill Lireth without killing Caden?

Maybe, Gedrith said. *The Enclave would rather imprison Lireth, but I fear that capturing her alive will be impossible without help. We're outnumbered and she won't be taken without a fight.*

Do you think Lord D'Lance will kill her, or do you think he'll try to force her into a bond as he did with the others?

I don't know.

Mina chewed her lower lip in thought. *I have an idea, but I don't know if it will work. It would rely on Lord D'Lance using his magic, and there's no guarantee he will.*

What is it?

If we can get Lireth's attention on us long enough for Lord D'Lance to use his magic on her, then we can kill him and take her captive.

The only way that plan works is if Lord D'Lance does what we want. How do we ensure he does?

We offer him something he wants.

What is that?

Caden.

16

Caden held on tightly as Lireth sped through the sky toward the castle. Lord D'Lance had joined the fray, and he'd brought a host of his riders with him. Upon seeing him, Lireth immediately ceased fighting Mina's dragon and turned her focus upon the Dominion Lord. Caden didn't blame her. He hated Lord D'Lance as well, and the opportunity to see him fall was too tempting to pass.

Stay alert, Lireth said. *Lord D'Lance has learned to use dark magic and he does not hesitate to use it.*

Caden gritted his teeth, remembering how the man had tried to kill him. *I'm well aware of what he's capable of.*

Lord D'Lance rode on the back of a green dragon. He stood without support as if he were part of the dragon itself, and he wore black plate armor that covered him from the neck down. He didn't wear a helmet, and his long black hair whipped freely behind him. If his hair wasn't moving, Caden imagined he could be nothing more than a statue.

Lireth roared in challenge and flapped her wings harder, picking up the pace. Caden drew his sword despite not having the reach of hitting anything and watched the distance close between them. The green dragon issued its own roar and a billowing cloud of yellow gas poured out from its mouth. Lireth banked to the left and flapped her right wing, sending the cloud backward into Lord D'Lance. The yellow gas swept around an invisible barrier that surrounded the Dominion Lord and the wind blew it away.

What is that stuff?

Poisonous gas, Lireth replied. *It'll burn your flesh if it touches you.*

And I thought fire was bad.

Lireth circled to the rear of the dragon, but another rider swooped in the way. Lireth went up, cracking the rider's dragon in the head with her thick tail. The blow knocked the dragon's head to the side and it careened out of control. When she turned back toward Lord D'Lance, his dragon was on top of her. It grabbed onto Lireth's horns and jerked violently. Her neck undulated and Caden fell backward, slamming his back on her hard scales. He coughed and forced himself to sit up, then jabbed his sword at the dragon. He misjudged the distance and the sword stabbed nothing but the air.

Lord D'Lance looked down at him and glared. His hands moved in odd patterns and his mouth moved silently. The air rippled briefly and then lightning began flickering between his fingers. Before he could do anything with the magic, Lireth shook her head free and pulled her wings in, free falling a few feet. She unfurled them and caught the air, spiraling a few times before shooting back up at the green dragon.

She crashed bodily into the beast and used her

front claws to latch onto the dragon's throat. Blood splattered Lireth and Caden both as scales and flesh ripped free. Lireth snapped her jaws onto the dragon's wound and jolted her head back and forth, tearing the flesh further. The green dragon gurgled an anguished cry and its wings slackened.

Watch out! Caden warned.

Lord D'Lance unleashed his spell. Several lightning bolts flashed forth from his hands, all of them striking Lireth. Her body spasmed as the projectiles hit her, but she didn't make a sound. That impressed Caden. Lireth unhooked her mouth from the green dragon and winged backward. The dragon plummeted to the ground, Lord D'Lance still on its back. Lireth dived, following after the dead beast.

Lord D'Lance leaped through the air before the dragon collided into the ground with a thunderous crash, landing unharmed atop the rubble of a building. Lireth opened her jaws and unleashed a torrent of flames, but they sizzled from existence as they struck his invisible barrier.

Caden gripped the hilt of his blade, preparing to take the fight to the ground. As he shifted his legs to jump down, a shadow passed overhead. He looked up in time to see Mina dangling from her dragon's claw, her right foot outstretched. It connected with the side of his head, and pain exploded from his brow down to his neck. The force pushed him off Lireth's back and he fell a few feet before slamming facedown onto the rubble at Lord D'Lance's feet.

He gasped, trying to force the breath back into his lungs. He heard Lireth roar and the sounds of battle, but they sounded faint, as if they were far away. Someone rolled him over and the darkness that threatened to consume him was held at bay.

Lord D'Lance looked into his eyes.

"You've done more to irritate me than most," he said lowly.

Above them, Lireth and Mina's dragon battled, but he didn't see Mina anywhere. Air filled his lungs, and he slowly became aware that things had taken a turn for the worse. His body sagged as his strength abruptly left. He'd completely forgotten about Lord D'Lance's rune.

"What were you hoping to accomplish, Caden? Did you think you could defeat me? You're nothing more than a cockroach meant for the bottom of my boot. You've destroyed my city for nothing. Now I'm going to destroy your dragon and make you watch."

"You can't kill her," Caden whispered harshly. "She's stronger than you."

"Who said I was going to kill her? There is more than one way to destroy a dragon."

Lord D'Lance gripped Caden's face, his fingers hard as steel.

"You do not want to miss this."

With his other hand, Lord D'Lance pointed to Lireth and began muttering words that made

Caden's skin crawl. He tried to lift his arm to strike the Dominion Lord, but his muscles refused to obey. He watched helplessly as Lireth slowly became ensnared by Lord D'Lance's magic. Wispy white tendrils stretched from his hand and into the sky, wrapping around Lireth's body. As the tendrils touched her, her movements became sluggish. Caden could feel her strength flowing through him and into the Dominion Lord.

A group of Lord D'Lance's dragon riders arrived, forcing Mina's dragon to retreat. He fled, disappearing into the smoke above the still burning city. Lord D'Lance clenched his hand into a fist and Lireth began to descend. She roared and thrashed against the magic, but it didn't help. Lord D'Lance proved to be the more powerful of the two.

Caden's eyes watered. He did not know what Lord D'Lance had planned for her, but he knew it wasn't good. His own body refused to obey him, leaving him unable to help his master. Who knew where Bast was, and the draman were probably pillaging the city. Where were Lireth's brethren? Had they all died? Their plan seemed foolproof, but it shattered like broken glass in front of his eyes.

If only there was something he could do, or someone who could help. But there wasn't. There was nobody, and he was at the mercy of a maniacal tyrant.

"Just kill me and get it over with," he begged.

"Your fate will not be so easy," Lord D'Lance said.

By the time Lireth's body touched the ground, she was completely immobile. Lord D'Lance released Caden's face and walked over to the dragon, standing in front of her head. He laid a hand on her snout.

This was it. This was the end, and it was nothing like Caden had imagined it would be. Something caught his eye; a sliver of movement among the rubble. Was he seeing things, or was that …

Mina.

17

Mina crouched among the rubble of a ruined building. Her crazy idea had worked, for the most part, and now Caden was at the mercy of Lord D'Lance. What she had not expected, however, was that the Dominion Lord could deal with Caden and Lireth at the same time—all on his own.

He was more powerful than she expected, and now her plan was slightly astray. Instead of delivering Caden to Lord D'Lance and Lireth swooping in to rescue him, thereby taking over his focus, he had them both ensnared by magic.

This isn't going to work, she told Gedrith.

Why not?

Lord D'Lance has them both captive.

That is good. It will rid us of both.

Mina looked at Caden's prone form and couldn't help but feel a little guilty. She knew he was her enemy now, but that didn't mean she had to let him die.

If Lord D'Lance dies, does his magic fade?

I don't know, Gedrith replied.

I have a clear path to him, but if I kill him and his spells end, we may lose the chance to capture Lireth.

That's a risk we'll have to take. Our orders

were to kill Lord D'Lance.

I know, but which of them is the bigger threat?

Gedrith didn't reply. She knew Lireth could wreak more havoc than Lord D'Lance, but the dragon technically wasn't her responsibility. She shifted her eyes between the two enemies, struggling briefly before deciding.

She was going to kill Lord D'Lance.

The laughter of Thais and Lord Klodian echoed in her mind, and it dawned on her that she might not be able to kill him, that she might not even be able to get near him before he ended her existence.

Trust your training, Gedrith said. *Stop listening to your doubts.*

He was right, she knew that, but it wasn't easy to ignore the thoughts. They were strong and persuasive. Mina tightened her grip on the hilt of her sword and took a deep breath.

Get ready, she warned, but she was also talking to herself. She flicked her eyes to the sky. Gedrith was nowhere to be seen. Mina emerged from the rubble slowly, careful of where she stepped. Lord D'Lance was in front of Lireth, his hand on her snout. White tendrils of smoke were wrapped around the dragon, keeping her from moving. Lireth's fiery gaze locked on the Dominion Lord, but Mina knew the dragon saw her.

With each step, Mina's heart hammered louder in her ears. Only a few steps away, she lifted her sword above her head and grabbed the hilt with both hands. Her strike needed to be precise, but her hands tremored. She'd never killed anyone before, at least not with her own hands.

Calm yourself.

Mina inhaled a deep breath and held it. Her hands steadied, and she lunged forward, driving the blade in a downward motion, aiming for Lord D'Lance's exposed neck. Time slowed, and she watched the tip of the blade as it drew nearer.

Without even looking back, Lord D'Lance swung his right hand behind his head, slapping her sword wide. Her momentum was thrown off and she staggered to the left, her sword chopping the air harmlessly. She quickly recovered and whirled around to face Lord D'Lance. He turned his attention to her and smiled.

"You're just as foolish as Caden, so you must be one of his. Do you not realize I have the power of a dragon flowing through my veins?"

He moved so quickly that Mina's eyes barely registered a blur of motion before agony exploded throughout her chest. She flew back several feet and crashed into something hard. It took her a moment to register it was the remnants of a stone wall. Lord D'Lance began laughing, a deranged look on his face.

Mina gritted her teeth against the pain and stood. Lord D'Lance strode toward her, Lireth and Caden still unmoving. Mina brought her sword up and stepped forward to meet him, but she knew she couldn't beat him. He was more powerful than her with his magic alone, and now that he had Lireth's strength, she had lost all hope. But she was still going to fight. Perhaps her sanity had left, or perhaps it had never truly been there to begin with.

She jabbed her sword at an angle, trying to hit him in the neck again, but he batted it away. Mina jabbed a second time with the same result. With her third attempt, Lord D'Lance grabbed the blade with his bare hand and snarled foreign words. The metal of her blade drooped and then turned to liquid, splattering on the ground. Mina's eyes widened in shock. She threw the hilt at him and it struck his chest plate, clanging loudly but doing no harm.

Mina blinked, and Lord D'Lance was directly in front of her. He wrapped his hand around her neck and squeezed, choking her. She gasped and tried to break free of his grasp, but his hold was firm.

Help me! She screamed through the bond. She could feel Gedrith's presence, and it was the only thing that kept her from giving up.

"I don't need you, but I want your dragon," Lord D'Lance said. "Tell him to come to me."

"No," Mina rasped.

"You will if you want to live. Call him here. Now." He squeezed harder.

I will not let him kill you, Gedrith's voice filled her mind. He sent an image to her, and she knew exactly what to do. She could hear the flapping of his wings, and she knew the moment he came into view, because Lord D'Lance's gaze looked up to the sky. Her throat was warm, quickly becoming hot. Mina could see Gedrith's reflection in Lord D'Lance's eyes, and she held on to consciousness despite the blackness closing in around her.

Her lips parted, and she whispered, "The Enclave … sends … their regards."

The burning in her throat overwhelmed her and she opened her mouth as if to shout, but instead of her anguished cry, flames spewed forth. A fiery torrent washed over Lord D'Lance and he released her, screaming and staggering backward. The sickly smell of burnt flesh stung Mina's nostrils, but the flames continued unabated, bathing the Dominion Lord so fully that she could see nothing but fire.

Finally, the blaze died and the burning in her throat faded. She fell to her knees, overcome with weakness. Lord D'Lance was lying on the ground, writhing and crying out. He was somehow still alive. Mina crawled over to Caden and took his sword, then got on her feet and stumbled over to where Lord D'Lance was and stood over him. The man's face was burned so badly he was unrecognizable.

With no hesitation, Mina swung the sword down, separating his head from his body, and then she promptly turned away and vomited. She wiped the back of her hand across her lips and looked at Lireth. The tendrils of smoke still bound the dragon in place, but she thrashed about, trying to get free.

His magic still holds, she said as Gedrith landed nearby.

I see that. It will make our task easier.

Are you really going to take her back to the Enclave? You could kill her instead. It would ensure she never poses a threat again.

Although you are right, I will not kill her. She will face the Enclave for her crimes and be imprisoned for the rest of her life. What do you want to do with that one?

Mina turned to look at Caden. For a moment, she thought he was dead, but then she saw his chest rising and falling and realized he was only unconscious.

If Lireth is as ingrained in his mind as I fear, then we must keep them separated. He will face the same punishment as his master. Imprisonment.

A wise decision. With Lireth in the desert and Caden here, the distance will be too far for them to communicate. It doesn't break their bond, but it is just as effective.

How will we get Lireth to the Enclave?

Only one of my brethren fell in battle, so we will carry her. We need to make haste while her forces are in disarray, lest her minions try to free her.

Mina nodded, still looking at Caden.

Where should we take him?

I know a place.

18

Caden opened his eyes and slowly became aware of his surroundings. He was in a dimly lit room with stone walls. An iron gate, a cell door, was closed and sconces on the walls outside of the cell illuminated the space. He groaned as he sat up and noticed he was on the floor. His wrists were shackled, the chains connected to rings in the floor, and he had little movement. As his mind was putting it all together, he realized he wasn't alone.

"I was beginning to wonder if you'd ever wake up."

There was no mistaking her voice. It was as rooted in his mind as Lireth was.

"Mina," he said. "Where are we? What happened?"

She was leaning against the wall to his left, her arms crossed over her chest.

"You lost," she replied. "And so did Lord D'Lance."

"Lireth killed him?"

Mina laughed scornfully. "Hardly. Thanks to your rune, Lord D'Lance was able to draw on Lireth's strength through you. He almost killed me. Probably would have if it wasn't for Gedrith."

"Your dragon?"

She nodded. Caden looked around the room, but there wasn't much to see. He could feel Lireth's presence in his mind, but it was muted, as if a thick cloth was covering their connection. If what Mina said was true, then his master was defeated. He hesitated to ask, but he needed to know.

"Where is Lireth?"

"She's being taken to the Enclave for judgement."

"Will they kill her?"

"No. Gedrith says they will lock her up. She'll die of old age in an underground cave."

At least she's alive, Caden thought. He held his hands up and jingled the chains.

"Any chance I'm getting out of these?"

"No."

"What is this place?"

"This is Lord Culver's dungeon. I told him Lord Klodian transferred you here for crimes against the High Prince. You'll never see daylight again."

Caden silently digested her words. He was a prisoner, and Lireth was being taken somewhere else. Whose cruel idea was it to separate them so far from each other? Would he be able to sense her from such a distance, or would her presence shrink until she was nothing more than a memory? The uncertainty was going to make him sick.

"I'm sorry for what I said before. I'm sure you regret aiding Lord Klodian with killing all those dragons now that you know they aren't mindless animals."

Mina pushed off the wall and approached, kneeling in front of him.

"If you were free and Lireth wasn't, would you try to help her escape?"

"If you and your dragon were in the same situation, would you?"

"Our situations are not the same," Mina said. "Lireth is wicked. She's brainwashed you into blindly following her. Do you not see that?"

Caden smiled at her despite the turmoil of emotions raging within him. "You don't know her like I do. You think she is evil, but I know she is kind. She saved me and gave me a place among her draman. No one has ever accepted me as I am like she has."

"I did."

"That's not what I meant."

"Then perhaps you should say what you mean. You'll have plenty of time to learn how to do that in here."

"Your dragon has changed you. The way you hold yourself, the way you speak … you are not the girl I met."

"Did you prefer that I stayed the same? A meek slave, always bending to the will of others?"

"No, never that. I just wish that things had gone differently between us. If I would have told you that

I no longer wanted to leave the Thophate, you would never have asked Lord Klodian to send me away. Perhaps if I had never left …"

"I told you before that our destinies may be entwined, but they are not united. Whether or not you stayed would not have changed that. Avera had other plans for me."

Caden found it difficult to accept that she truly believed that, but he knew it was futile to argue the point.

"So you leave me here and go … where? What will you do now that Lord D'Lance is dead?"

"That's none of your business," Mina replied. She leaned closer to him. "You were a good man once. Maybe you will be again. Once Lireth is out of your mind, I hope that your sanity will return. If you can find a way to remove yourself from her bond, do it. That'll be the only way you get out of here."

Caden stared into her blue eyes and longed to touch her, but he didn't dare try. She returned his stare with equal intensity, but neither of them spoke. Finally, she leaned in and kissed him on the lips. He closed his eyes and savored the moment, which ended too soon. Mina pulled away from him and stood up.

"Goodbye, Caden."

And with that, she pushed open the cell door and walked away. A guard stepped into view. He closed the gate and locked it, then returned to his post. Caden sighed and laid back down on the floor, staring at the ceiling. Mina told him end his bond with Lireth, but he would not do that. If anything, he was determined to strengthen it and find a way to escape.

One step at a time, he told himself. *One step at a time.*

—

As Mina left the dungeon, she had to force herself to ignore the pleadings of her heart. Caden was her enemy as long as he was bonded to Lireth, and she held no reservations about locking him up. It was for his own good as much as it was to keep the world safe. Still, the thought that she might never see him again gave her pause.

He'd asked what her plans were, but she didn't tell him because she didn't want him to know where she was in the unlikely event that he ever managed to get out of the prison. Now that the tyrant Lord D'Lance was no longer a threat, she was free to do as she pleased. Her odd relationship with Lord Klodian had ended on a sour note, so she couldn't go back to the Thophate, especially not with a dragon.

Perhaps she would return to the Enclave and continue training as a rider with Areg. Or perhaps she wouldn't. Nothing was set in stone, and she liked the idea of having the free will to do anything she dreamed of … or nothing at all.

She left Lord Culver's castle behind and trekked into the grain fields where Gedrith and his brethren awaited her. Lireth was there as well, still magically bound, and Mina climbed onto Gedrith's back.

All is well? He asked.

Yes. We are all set to leave.

Good. I miss the desert.

Mina smiled and held on tightly as the dragon lifted off the ground. Between him and the remaining silver dragons, they were able to carry Lireth in their claws. They gained altitude and rose higher, then turned south toward The Long Sands, toward the Enclave. Mina closed her eyes and let the wind whip her hair about, enjoying the sensation of flying.

It felt good to be free.

THE END

ABOUT THE AUTHOR

Richard Fierce is a fantasy and space opera author. He's been writing since childhood, but began publishing in 2007. Since then, he's written multiple novels and short stories.

In 2000, Richard won Poet of the Year for his poem *The Darkness*. He's also one of the creative brains behind the Allatoona Book Festival, a literary event in Acworth, Georgia.

A recovering retail worker, he now works in the tech industry when he's not busy writing.

He's married and has three step-daughters (pray for him), a grandson, three dogs (huskies!), four cats, and two ferrets. He basically has a zoo.

His love affair with fantasy was born in high school when a friend's mother gave him a copy of *Dragons of Spring Dawning* by Margaret Weis and Tracy Hickman.